THE FISHERMAN UNDER THE SEA

by Miyoko Matsutani • illustrated by Chihiro Iwasaki

English Version by Alvin Tresselt

This book was translated from Urashima Taro,
originally published by Kaisei Sha Publishing Company,
Tokyo, Japan. The American edition has been arranged
through Nippon Shuppan Hanbai K.K., Tokyo.

Parents' Magazine Press • New York

Copyright (c) 1969 by Parents' Magazine Press
All rights reserved
Printed in the United States of America
Library of Congress Catalog Card Number: 69-13126

In a time long ago there lived a handsome
young man named Taro Urashima. He was
a fisherman, and he lived in a village
near the sea. Each day he put out in his
boat to catch fish to sell in the market.
And in this way he earned his living.

It so happened one day he sailed out to sea as usual, but in the whole day he did not catch so much as one fish. Returning that night he came upon a group of noisy children gathered around a little turtle. They were having great fun, banging on the poor creature's shell and swinging it by the tail.

Taro's heart was touched with pity when he saw this,
and he begged the children to release the turtle.
Somewhat ashamed of their unkind behavior, the children
handed the turtle to him and ran off down the beach.
The fisherman now looked more closely at the turtle
and was surprised to discover that it was like no other
he had ever seen. Its shell glowed with the pure colors
of the rainbow. At length he put the turtle down by the
edge of the water, and the creature quickly crawled
into the protecting waves. Taro watched.
Then, just as he turned to leave, the turtle appeared
and solemnly nodded its head as if to say *thank you.*

The next day Taro set out again to fish. "Let us hope that today brings greater fortune than yesterday," he said as he lowered his nets into the water.

But at that instant a huge turtle appeared at the edge of the boat. Bowing his head he spoke to the startled fisherman. "I have come to thank you for saving the life of a small turtle," he said. "I have been told by my master, the King of the Sea, to take you down to his Dragon Palace so that he may thank you also. Would you be so kind as to climb upon my back?"

Taro was so surprised by this strange request that he did not think to do otherwise. He jumped from his boat and quickly seated himself on the turtle's back, slippery with sea moss. Slowly the creature turned around, then dove down, down into the blue-green water of the sea.

Taro was surrounded by beautifully colored fish of every shape and size, and strange seaweeds floated in the water about him. Soon they were in an underwater land of great mountains and valleys. Then in the distance the shining walls of a palace appeared. It was the Dragon Palace of the King of the Sea.

On through groves of coral trees they went, while brilliant fish darted in and out among the red and pink branches like birds. At last they arrived at the great gate of the palace itself. The building with its coral pillars and a roof of delicate sea shells shimmered in the rippling water.

Taro Urashima gasped with astonishment. Never had the simple fisherman ever seen anything so beautiful. Servants appeared at the doorway to welcome him, and to the sound of distant music he was ushered into the halls of the palace.

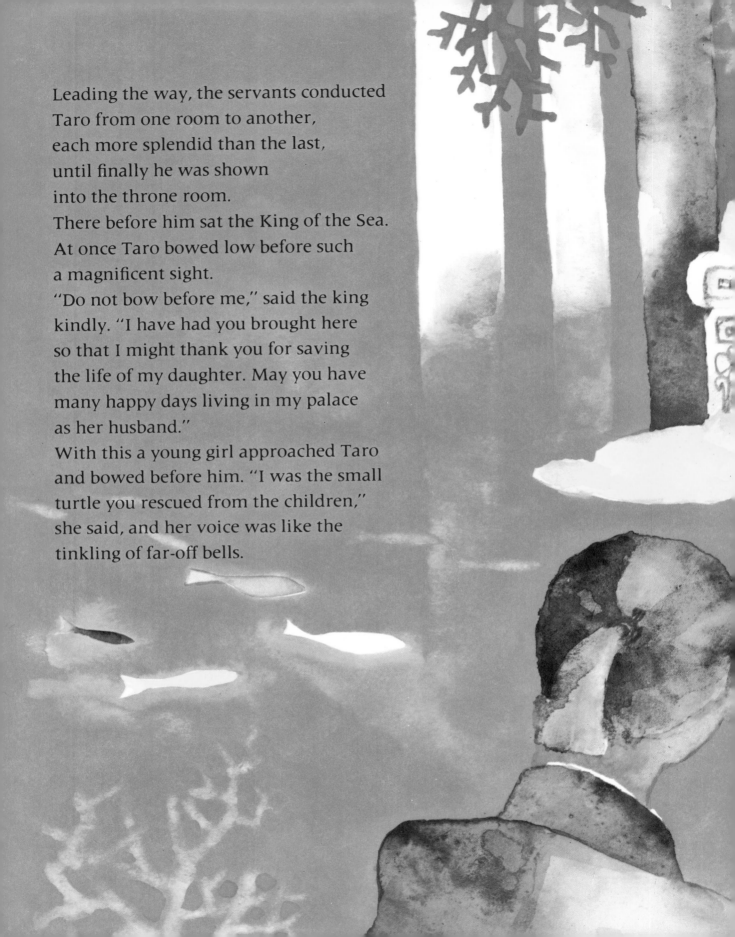

Leading the way, the servants conducted
Taro from one room to another,
each more splendid than the last,
until finally he was shown
into the throne room.
There before him sat the King of the Sea.
At once Taro bowed low before such
a magnificent sight.
"Do not bow before me," said the king
kindly. "I have had you brought here
so that I might thank you for saving
the life of my daughter. May you have
many happy days living in my palace
as her husband."
With this a young girl approached Taro
and bowed before him. "I was the small
turtle you rescued from the children,"
she said, and her voice was like the
tinkling of far-off bells.

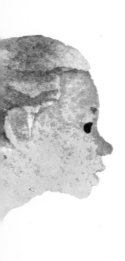

Taro was speechless before such beauty. The princess moved with the suppleness of a blade of sea grass waving in the water, and her smile was as gentle as the sea waves on a calm day.

Seeing the question in Taro's eyes she said, "I had never left my home here in the Dragon Palace, and I was curious to see the people who live on the land. I changed myself into a little turtle and swam to the shore of your country. But, alas, I had no sooner crawled up on the beach when I was found by those children. If you had not rescued me from them, I am afraid my fate would have been a sad one." Before Taro could answer she went on. "But I forget. You must be hungry after your long journey."

She waved her hand and there suddenly appeared a table laden with all manner of delicious foods.

In all his born days Taro had never tasted such food. The
rice wine was the color of amber washed up by the sea,
the fish was delicately flavored with strange herbs, and
the pastries were as light and fragile as snowflakes.
The dishes were of the finest gold and silver, and the
food was served in lacquer bowls of glowing red. Taro
had scarcely begun to eat when the princess waved her
hand again. At once beautiful dancing girls appeared
to entertain him, and the sound of music filled the hall.

When the feast was over, the princess took him by the hand and led him on and on through the countless rooms of the palace. Presently they came to a large window looking out upon broad fields.

It was spring, and Taro could see the farmers busily planting the young rice in the flooded paddies. But even as he looked the plants grew instantly, and the countryside changed from the fresh green of springtime to the richer green of midsummer. He had no sooner marveled at this when he saw that the rice plants were bent over, heavy with the weight of ripened grain, and autumn had come. Scarcely was the grain harvested when the snows of winter were falling. In no more than a minute a whole year had appeared before his eyes!

And so the time passed for Taro in the Dragon Palace beneath the sea. Never had he been so happy. The lovely princess became his wife and his constant companion. There were servants at his beck and call to fulfill his slightest wish. One day followed another, and whether it was real or just a dream he could not tell.

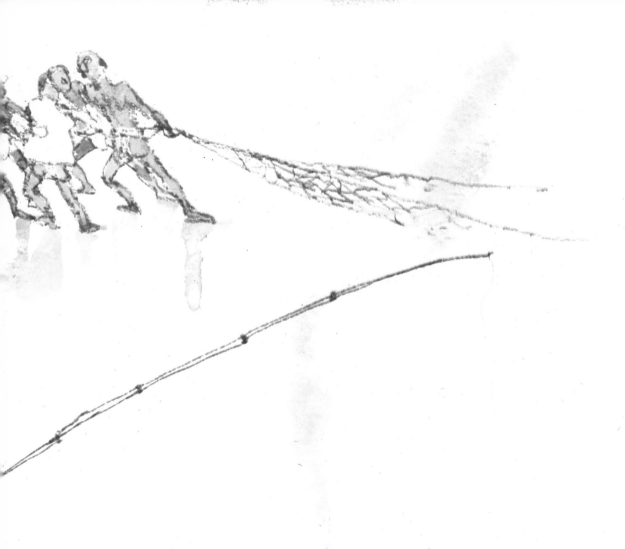

But one day in a quiet moment, Taro suddenly recalled his fishing boat,
and the joy of pulling nets filled with fish up out of the sea. He
thought of his mother and his friends in the village. How he would
like to see them all, and tell of his life here in the palace!
Going to the princess he told her of his desire to see his village
once more.

She tried to persuade him to stay,
but at last, seeing that Taro was
determined to go, she sadly agreed
to let him leave. "But take this
with you," she said, handing him
a box of finest red lacquer.
"As long as you keep this safe,
you will always be able to come
back to me." Then she paused.
"But remember—you must never
open the box to see what is in it."
Taro embraced his wife and
assured her that he would return.
Then, with the blessings of the
King of the Sea, he set out
from the Dragon Palace.

Once more Taro mounted the back of the old turtle and began the journey to his own land. Quickly the shining walls of the palace disappeared from view. Through the valleys and past the mountains they went, then up, up to the surface of the sea, and there before him Taro saw again the houses of his village beside the sea.

He thanked the turtle for his safe trip,
then ran up the beach toward his village.
But something was wrong! The familiar
shape of the mountain behind the village
was still there, but the streets and houses
all looked different. Taro wandered
through the strange streets to where his
house should have been, but there was a
building he had never seen before.
Going up to a villager he asked, "Is this
not the place where Taro Urashima lives?"
The man looked at him with surprise.
"Taro Urashima's house rotted and fell
down many years ago," he replied.

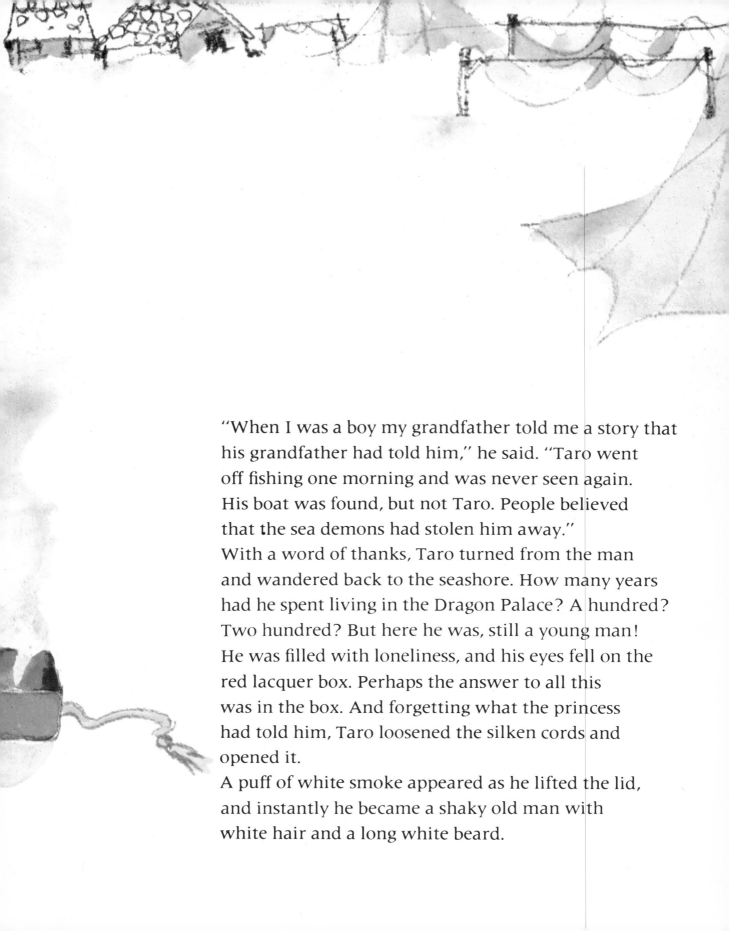

"When I was a boy my grandfather told me a story that his grandfather had told him," he said. "Taro went off fishing one morning and was never seen again. His boat was found, but not Taro. People believed that the sea demons had stolen him away."

With a word of thanks, Taro turned from the man and wandered back to the seashore. How many years had he spent living in the Dragon Palace? A hundred? Two hundred? But here he was, still a young man! He was filled with loneliness, and his eyes fell on the red lacquer box. Perhaps the answer to all this was in the box. And forgetting what the princess had told him, Taro loosened the silken cords and opened it.

A puff of white smoke appeared as he lifted the lid, and instantly he became a shaky old man with white hair and a long white beard.

Then faintly from over the water he heard the sad voice
of the princess. "Oh, Taro, Taro, my husband, my beloved.
You promised me you would never open the box," she cried.
"It was your life I had shut up so that you would never grow
old. Farewell, Taro, farewell."
And the voice of the princess was lost in the sound of the
sea waves crashing on the shore at the old man's feet.

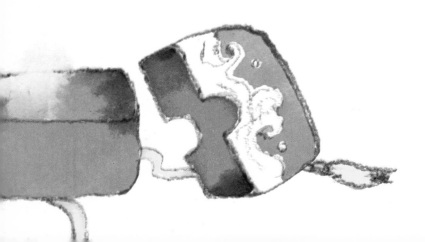